This book belongs to:
_____

YOGA BEAR
Yoga for Youngsters

by
KAREN PIERCE,
RYT

illustrated by
PAULA BRINKMAN

NORTHWORD PRESS
Chanhassen, Minnesota

The publisher would like to thank the following consultants:
Kelly Prestia, MSEd, OTR/L and Laura Erdman-Luntz, MA, RYT.
And a very special thank you to our little "yoga bears":
Abi, Amy, Angela, Elke, Ethan, Felix, Helena, Jacob, Jake,
Kameron, Mackenzie, Oscar, Serena, and Sierra.

The illustrations were created using a technical pen, Luma inks, and colored pencil
The text and display type were set in ITC Garamond and Chalkboard
Composed in the United States of America
Designed by Lois A. Rainwater
Edited by Aimee Jackson

Photography © 2004 by NorthWord Press. All rights reserved.
Text © 2004 by Karen Pierce
Illustrations © 2004 by Paula Brinkman

Books for Young Readers
NorthWord Press
18705 Lake Drive East
Chanhassen, MN 55317
www.northwordpress.com

Library of Congress Cataloging-in-Publication Data

Pierce, Karen Behan, date.
Yoga bear : yoga for youngsters
p. cm.
ISBN 1-55971-897-8 (hc with dust jacket)
1. Yoga, Hatha, for children—Juvenile literature. I. Brinkman, Paula. II. Title.
RA781.7.P546 2004
613.7'046'083—dc22   2004002890

I would like to express my gratitude
to my friends and family for their unconditional love.
Especially to my amazing husband, Dan,
who has supported me in everything I do;
and my little yoginis, Danielle and Timmy,
who were always willing participants.

Special thanks to Joanna Cole,
who listened to my dreams during our yoga sessions
and encouraged me to put them down on paper.

To my teachers past,
present, and
future—Namaste

—K.P.

Dear Parents and Educators

CONGRATULATIONS! You are helping your child develop a strong, healthy body. Yoga is a great form of exercise for children of any age. *Yoga Bear: Yoga for Youngsters* is geared to two- to six-year-olds, but you can start introducing yoga poses to children as young as eighteen months. Children of this age learn by imitation, so feel free to jump in and join the fun. Not only will you set a good example, you may discover you enjoy yoga as much as your child does. Yoga is an activity that the whole family can enjoy together!

What is yoga?

Yoga is a gentle, non-competitive form of exercise that works the whole body. Yoga is a philosophy. It is not about attaining perfect poses, it is about creating a state of healthy balance and well-being in which the body and mind can function at their best.

Yoga Bear introduces yoga to your child by exploring and imitating nature through twenty-two postures. Many yoga poses are dedicated to nature and its creatures and reflect the interconnectedness of all things. Yoga practice usually includes breathing exercises and some period of meditation or relaxation at the end. The purpose of yoga is to unite the body, breath, mind, and spirit to create peace and balance. Yoga is also about fun and fitness!

Who can do yoga?

Yoga is for everyone! It is beneficial for children of all ages and physical abilities. Practicing and holding poses helps children develop muscle strength and flexibility, improve stamina and concentration, and build self-esteem.

Children with special needs

Yoga is particularly helpful for children with special needs or limited mobility. Yoga can help children who have Down Syndrome with muscle strengthening and weight management.

Yoga poses positively improve the muscle tone and balance of children with Cerebral Palsy. Children with ADD/ADHD respond to the relaxing effects of the poses, as well as the breathing exercises. This can reduce hyperactivity and improve concentration and memory. The overall effect is a sense of well-being and a relaxed state of body and mind. It is important to adapt the poses and create variations based on the physical and mental abilities of the individual. Regardless of the severity of the disability, yoga poses and breathing and relaxation techniques can help to improve motor development, develop body awareness, improve concentration, and stretch and strengthen the body, resulting in greater independence.

Getting started

Choose comfortable clothes and practice in bare feet on a non-slip surface such as a yoga mat, wood floor, or carpet. Young children should be supervised. The book includes instructions to help you and your child prepare and explore the poses. There are also variations to help adapt the poses to the individual abilities of the child. However, if your child encounters any difficulty, please discontinue and seek out an appropriate modification through a qualified teacher. Yoga Bear begins with a warm-up and ends with a wind-down. Active poses are performed in between.

Feel your roots grow as you stand in Mountain Pose.

MOUNTAIN POSE

Parent's Instructions: Stand with feet together, arms hanging at sides. Grow up through the top of the head toward the heavens while grounding the feet into the ground. Stand solid on a firm foundation—still, like the Mighty Mountain.

Benefits: Strengthens the back and improves posture.

Can you jump into Elephant's Trunk?

ELEPHANT'S TRUNK POSE

Parent's Instructions: Stand with feet wide apart and toes turned out slightly.
Bend the knees, allowing the tailbone to come to knee level. Keep the body weight in the heels and keep the spine straight.
Then draw the hands and elbows in together. Adapt by straightening the knees and separating the elbows.

Benefits: Strengthens the legs and arms and stretches the back and shoulders.

Can you dangle like the Triangle?

TRIANGLE POSE

Parent's Instructions: Stand with legs wide apart. With arms parallel to floor, turn one foot in the direction you will reach. Then tilt sideways in that direction while "windmilling" the hand to the foot and opposite hand to ceiling so that the arms are aligned vertically. Look up at ceiling. Adapt by reaching for the shin or ankle.

Benefits: Stretches and strengthens the legs, hips, and spine.

Look at me. I'm a Tree! Can you shake your leaves in the breeze?

TREE POSE

Parent's Instructions: Stand with feet together. Imagine the feet are the roots of a tree growing deep into the Earth. Shift weight to one leg and slide other foot up so heel is against thigh and knee is turned out. Stretch arms upward in a "V" like tree limbs growing to the sun. Adapt by keeping foot lower on leg and arms down with hands together in Prayer Position.

Benefits: This balancing pose strengthens the legs and stretches the inner thighs.

How do you suppose Dog Pose goes? Can you wag your tail?

DOWNWARD FACING DOG POSE

Parent's Instructions: Kneel on hands and knees. Straighten the legs so the hips are jackknifed to the ceiling and the body looks like an inverted "V." The head is relaxed between the arms. Press the heels and hands into floor like a dog stretching its front legs and wagging its tail in the air. Adapt by bending the knees.

Benefits: This powerful pose energizes the body, as well as stretches and strengthens the arms and legs.

Does
a Lion
snore,
or
does he
roar?

Parent's Instructions: Kneel on floor with knees and feet together. Lower hips to heels and place hands on thighs. Bring chin to chest, widen eyes and stick out tongue, reaching tongue toward chin. Then roar like a lion! Adapt by sitting on a block or blanket.

Benefits: Stretches the thighs, opens lungs and throat, and strengthens voice.

Sing a
tune
to the
Crescent
Moon.

CRESCENT MOON POSE

Parent's Instructions: Kneel on knees, stretch one leg out to side with foot down and toes facing front.
Slide arm down leg, reaching toward same ankle, and reach opposite arm up toward the ceiling, then letting it drop over ear.

Benefits: Opens the ribs and stretches the hips and the muscles around the spine.

Arch your back, scary Cat.

Can you moo like a Cow would do?

CAT POSE
Parent's Instructions: Kneel on all fours with hips over the knees, and pull the chin to chest, rounding the back. Tuck tailbone under, becoming an angry cat!

Benefits: Stretches the back and strengthens the abdominals.

COW POSE
Parent's Instructions: Kneel on hands and knees, bring head up as the spine relaxes. Expand the chest and let the back sag like an old cow.

Benefits: Strengthens the back and stretches the abdominals.

Is that a shark fin, or a Dolphin?

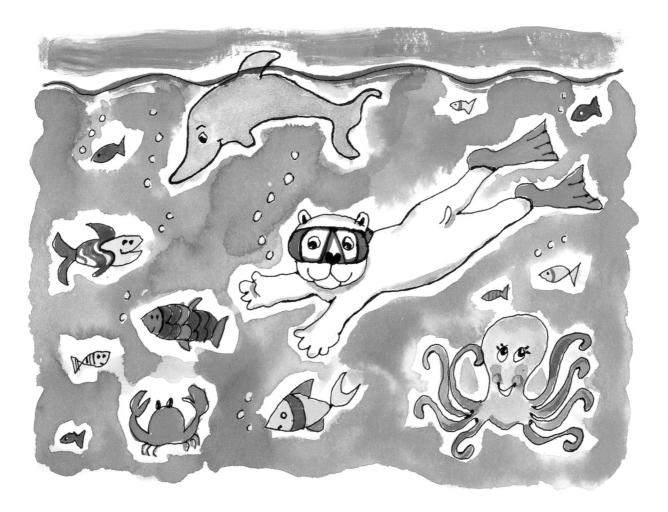

DOLPHIN POSE

Parent's Instructions: Kneel on all fours with back rounded. Interlace fingers around the back of head and place top of head to floor. Round the back up toward the ceiling like the dolphin pressing his dorsal fin up through the ocean water.

Benefits: Stretches the muscles along the spine.

Are you able to do the Table?

TABLE POSE

Parent's Instructions: While kneeling on all fours, simultaneously raise one leg and opposite arm parallel to the floor. Reach toes to back wall and fingers to front wall. Head is relaxed, eyes gazing at the floor next to hand.

Benefits: Improves balance and coordination and strengthens the back and abdominal muscles.

shhhhh

Quiet as a Mouse
in a cat-filled house.

MOUSE POSE

Parent's Instructions: Kneel on all fours and lower hips to heels.
Bring the forehead to the floor and lay arms on floor alongside the body. Get very small and quiet like a mouse.

Benefits: A resting pose that calms the body and mind and allows the body to come back into balance.

What's it like when a Cobra strikes?

COBRA POSE

Parent's Instructions: Lie facedown with legs together and toes pointed. Place hands under shoulders. Straighten the arms and lift chest off floor, slithering forward like a snake. With the hips on the floor, raise the head like the snake getting ready to strike. Adapt by resting on elbows instead of straight arms.

Benefits: Flexibility of the spine.

Ready, set, go! Shoot the Bow!

BOW POSE

Parent's Instructions: Lie facedown. Bend knees and reach back to clasp ankles with hands,
keeping knees together. Lift the chin and chest while simultaneously raising knees off floor, drawing toes to top of head
and arching the back like a bow. Adapt by keeping legs separated or by grabbing one leg at a time.

Benefits: Strengthens the muscles along the spine and opens the chest and shoulders.

Lie still awhile, Crocodile.

CROCODILE POSE

Parent's Instructions: Lie facedown with arms at sides and legs slightly apart. Imagine that you are floating down the river.

Benefits: This resting pose allows the body to come back into balance.

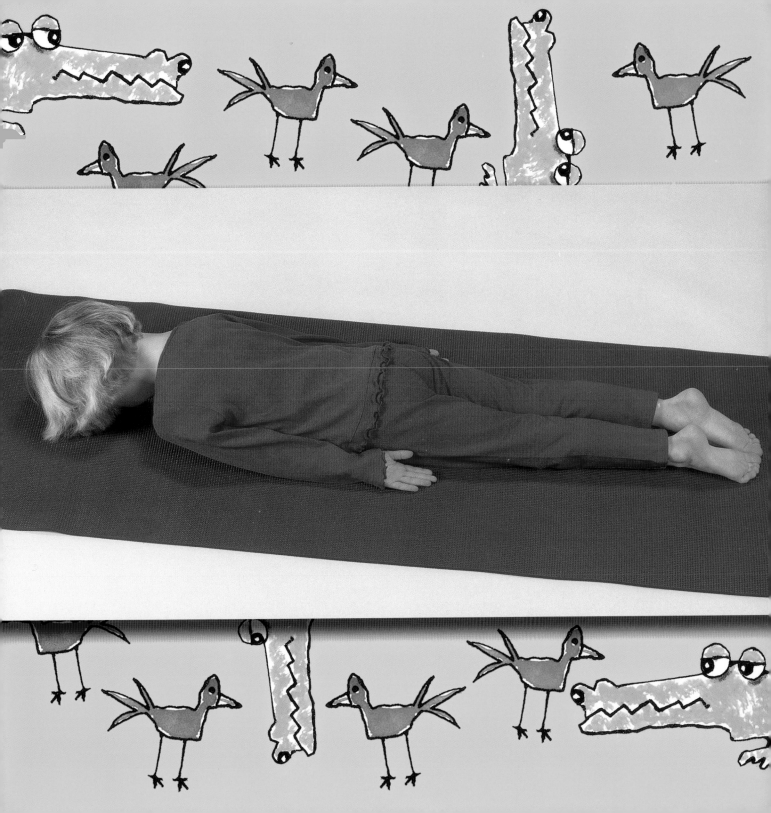

Squat like a Frog
and leap over a log!

FROG POSE

Parent's Instructions: Stand with feet hip-width apart and hands together in Prayer Position.
Turn feet out and bend knees, lowering the tailbone to the floor. Keep the spine straight. Place hands on floor.
Return to standing pose. Adapt by straightening the knees.

Benefits: Strengthens the legs and stretches the knees, hips, and groin.

How many volts are in a Thunderbolt?

THUNDERBOLT POSE

Parent's Instructions: Standing, raise your hands overhead with palms facing one another. Bend your knees so your thighs are almost parallel to the ground and your body is leaning forward slightly. It should look like you are sitting in an imaginary chair!

Benefits: Stretches shoulders and strengthens legs.

How high in the sky can you fly, Butterfly?

BUTTERFLY POSE

Parent's Instructions: Sit with knees bent and soles of feet together.
Keeping the spine straight with heels close to the body, let gravity gently pull the knees to floor.
Then flap the legs just like a butterfly waving its wings. Adapt by moving feet away from body.

Benefits: Stretches inner thighs and hips.

Rain
showers
bring
Lotus
flowers.

LOTUS POSE

Parent's Instructions: Sit on the floor. Place one foot on the opposite thigh, close to the lower belly.
Slide the other leg over, pressing that heel into the lower belly. Keep the knees as close to each other as possible. Adapt by sitting in simple seated pose with crossed legs, or by cradling one leg at a time in both arms and rocking it back and forth.

Benefits: Opens the hips while stretching knees and ankles.

Can you float like a Boat?

BOAT POSE

Parent's Instructions: Sit on the floor with legs straight, then lean back slightly as you raise your feet to eye level and stretch out arms alongside knees. Adapt by keeping knees bent or by placing one foot on the floor.

Benefits: This balancing pose strengthens the abdominals.

What's that on the rug?
Ick! It's a dead bug.

DEAD BUG POSE

Parent's Instructions: Lie on back and grab the insides of the feet. Flex the feet and bring the knees toward the chest.
Gently pull the feet down toward the floor so the shins are perpendicular, or vertical to the floor.
Be really still, like a dead bug. Adapt by grabbing the shins, or one leg at a time.

Benefits: Stretches the hips, legs, and groin.

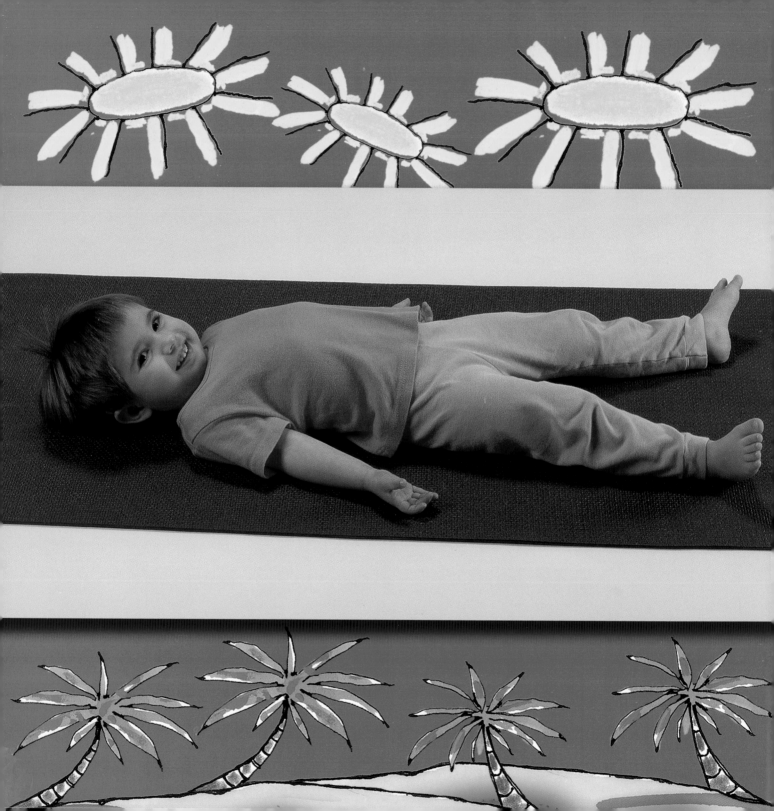

The sponge lives in the sea.
Let's float together, you and me!

SPONGE POSE

Parent's Instructions: Lie on the floor quietly and completely relaxed. Arms comfortable at sides with palms up, legs hip-width apart and feet turned out slightly. Soften the entire body and let it sink into the Earth. Breathe deeply, let go, completely relax, and open the heart. Adapt by bending knees with feet on the floor.

Benefits: Allows total relaxation.

KAREN PIERCE is the mother of two baby yoga bears. She has practiced yoga, meditation, and Eastern studies for nearly twenty years, seven of those years as a yoga teacher (registered through the National Yoga Alliance), as

well as fifteen years teaching in the fitness industry (certified aerobics instructor, pre/post-natal specialist, kickboxing instructor, and certified personal trainer). She has developed her own style, incorporating her specialties. Ms. Pierce lives in Newtown, Connecticut.

PAULA BRINKMAN is a graduate of the University of Connecticut. For many years she lived in New York City, working as a freelance illustrator. Her work has appeared in magazines and books, on greeting cards, menus, T-shirts, and other doodads. Ms. Brinkman lives in Key West, Florida, with her husband and daughter. Karen and Paula have been friends since elementary school.